Luro
Antiochia
Redi
Alexandria
Patremo
Seluria
Antiochia
Alepo
Zegar
Pireguch
Laodicia
Pos
Canficon
Famagusta
Aradus
Tortosa
Caron.
Le Dicha
Mebeg
Orrant fl.
Tripoli
Barim
Gelli
CASTOTIS
Mebeg
Besenas
Aman
Orom fl.
Biblus
CASTOIVS
Ems
Beritas
Julia
SIRIA
Asche
Sidon
Barudi
Anti libanus
Damasco
Tirus
Canami:
Cape
Gabalo
Erusa
Clecef
Aree
Cedar
Nephthalim
Libanus
COELE
GALLILÆA
Cesarea
Neue
Trachonitis
Cesarea
M: Seif
Rabbat
Erahilon
Corazim
Pella
Capitolis
BER
Hesbon
Modin
Samali

# THE HIDDEN TREASURES OF MY KINGDOM PALS
# THE TREASURE OF TRUST

## David

"Whenever I am afraid, I will trust in You."
*Psalms 56:3 (NKJV)*

ZOË LIFE PUBLISHING
*Words to Live By*

Canton, Michigan

**Published by:**
Zoe Life Publishing
P.O. Box 871066
Canton, MI 48111 USA

**Co-Authors:** Julie Page and Sabrina Adams
**Edited by:** Rhonda McTeer
**Illustrator:** Mike Motz

First U.S. Edition 2004

**Publisher's Cataloging-In-Publication Data**

Summary:
Three friends journey into the forest to search for treasure.  They are led by a rainbow to a chest filled with jewels. With the help of My Kingdom Pal ™, David, they soon discover the jewels they've found have words written on them and these words are truths from God.  They learn that, by applying these truths to their everyday lives, God will help them do extraordinary things.
by Julie Page and Sabrina Adams — 1st edition.

ISBN 09748251-0-7 Hardcover Edition

1. Children's Picture Book (age 3 – 8)
2. Parenting

Library of Congress Control Number:   2004095813

Printed in Korea

For current information about releases from Zoe Life Publishing, visit our web site:
http://www.zoelifepub.com

# Dedication

We dedicate this book to our children and grandchildren Lisa, Brittany, Eliya, Brantley, Kristy, Justin, Aaron and Jacob.  We thank God for entrusting us to love, care for and give to you the greatest gift of all—a strong spiritual heritage.

# Acknowledgements

This project has been a great partnership maximizing to the fullest extent the gifts God has placed in each one of us. Thanks to all who participated in any way.

### *My Kingdom Pals*

Mike McTeer                    Rhonda McTeer

For their loving creation of the My Kingdom Pal ™ Plush Bible Characters and commitment to put the word of God in the hands of children.  Also to Rhonda for her editorial support

### *Writers and Illustrator*

Julie Page
For her creativity, storyline and heart's desire to see every child fulfill their life's purpose

Sabrina Adams
For her vision for the book and contributions to the Parenting and Teachers Section

Pastor Jim Richter    Open Arms Lutheran Church, Belleville, MI
For continuous enthusiastic encouragement, prayer and his passionate commitment to pass on a solid spiritual heritage to future generations

Mike Motz
For his commitment to the project
and his creative brilliance in bringing each character from concept to reality

### *Proof Reader, Designer and Book Manufacturer*

Stephanie Gledhill
For your eye for detail

Shelly Makus
For skillfully laying out each page

Moshe Shor
Graphics International
For making our dreams of printing this book a reality

### *Special Thanks*

To our husbands, Richard, Brian, Mike and all the understanding spouses of everyone who participated in this project and an extra special thank you to Terri Evans and Laverne Slaughter, for their continuous enthusiasm, prayers, encouragement and support.

# Table of Contents

# Forward

After reading *The Treasure of Trust* and hearing about *The Hidden Treasures of My Kingdom Pals* series, all I can say is, "Thank you!" As a father, Pastor, and church leader, from the depth of my heart I say, "Thank you for some desperately needed help!"

The greatest charge that God has given parents, and those who support the work of parents, is to pass the knowledge of His love, character, commandments, and promises on to their children. *(Deuteronomy 6:4-7)* This knowledge of our loving God is not only the greatest charge God has given to parents, it is also the greatest gift that parents can give to their children. Knowledge of God unlocks a treasure chest of blessings for life ... but even more importantly ... it unlocks the treasure chest of blessings for eternity. *The Hidden Treasures of My Kingdom Pals"* is a tool and a weapon that helps parents, and those who support the work of parents, to fulfill this greatest charge and give this greatest gift in a creative, interesting, and fun way.

It seems strange in the forward of a children's book to talk about a tool and a weapon ... especially when the book is designed to be used with irresistible stuffed dolls called My Kingdom Pals™ ... but these two terms are what stick in my mind as I celebrate this first book *The Hidden Treasures of My Kingdom Pals* series by Julie Page and Sabrina Adams in conjunction with Mike and Rhonda McTeer. This book is first of all a fantastic tool. There is a genuine and growing desire among parents, and those who support the work of parents, to fulfill God's charge to pass on a spiritual heritage to their children. As news bytes show an unstable and often crumbling world, the desire to pass on the rock solid foundation of trust in God and values to the next generation grows stronger and stronger. But, parents are scrambling for practical tools they can use to pass on the faith. The stories and pictures found in *The Treasure of Trust* provide just such a practical tool. The book and the Kingdom Pal David provide a profound interactive teaching tool that will provide hours of teaching at just the right moment ... the teachable moment.

This book is also a weapon. The Bible teaches that "God is a Warrior." He battles for good and always wins over evil. He battles for the hearts of people, big and small alike, so that they might be rescued from sin, and death, and Satan and be with Him for now and for eternity. One serious look at the passion of Jesus Christ reinforces this undeniable truth. God has called every parent and every person who supports the work of parents to take up arms and join him in battling for the hearts and souls of our children. When the television is turned on - the battle rages. When our children step on to the playground - the battle rages. The battle is all around. We cannot ignore it. At stake are the hearts and souls of our children. In the midst of this battle Julie, Sabrina, Mike and Rhonda have come to our aid with an important weapon.

*The Treasure of Trust* is a gift that is destined along with the rest of the books in *The Hidden Treasures of My Kingdom Pals* series and the Kingdom Pals to become standard equipment in the tool boxes and arsenals of parents and all those who support the work of parents. Enjoy the book with the children God has entrusted to your care. It's fun!! But, don't underestimate its usefulness as you seek to fulfill your God-given responsibility to pass faith and values to the next generation.

> *"We will not hide them from their children;*
> *we will tell the next generation the praiseworthy deeds of the LORD,*
> *his power and the wonders he has done ...*
> *Then they will put their trust in God and would not forget his deeds but would keep his commands."*
> NIV, Psalm 78:4, 7

Jim Richter
Sr. Pastor, Open Arms Lutheran Church and Family Resource Center
Belleville, MI

# Introduction

*Train up a child in the way he should go: and when he is old, he will not depart from it.*
Proverbs 22:6

The "My Kingdom Pal™" Ministry was birthed out of a desire to help parents put the word of God in the hands of children. In this story, Kingdom Pal, David, will captivate your child as he leads them on a journey to discover the *Treasure of Trust*. You can learn more about "My Kingdom Pals" in the section "About the Kingdom Pals".

As parents, teachers and caregivers we have an awesome opportunity to impart blessings into the next generation. Within the being of every child is a seed that has the potential to change the world. It is our job to cultivate that seed, to water, to fertilize and to prune so at maturity that seed can blossom and fulfill the purposes and plans that God has established for that unique child. God has entrusted us with this great work. He has also given us His Word, the Bible to help us along the way. The purpose of this book is to present God's Word in a way that speaks to the heart of your child.

*The Hidden Treasures of My Kingdom Pals* Series is not your ordinary children's book series. The series will capture your child's heart and imagination. It will outfit you with tools to help you successfully navigate the complicated maze of raising productive, loving, capable children who have a personal relationship with God the Father through His son Jesus, a relationship based on trust, intimacy and sound biblical principles, so that when they grow into adulthood, they will not depart from the truth of God's word.

# How to Get the Most Out of This Book

*Such things were written in the Scriptures long ago to teach us. They give us hope and encouragement as we wait patiently for God's promises.*
Romans 15:4 NLT

**Read the end first.** The chapter, "Just for Parents, Teachers and Caregivers", will take you on a page by page journey through the "Treasure of Trust" and uncover the jewels that have been scattered throughout each illustration designed to encourage, uplift and edify your child.

**Do not try to read the entire story in just one sitting.** Linger over every page. Discuss with your child what they see and point out things they do not see. Spend time questioning, listening, informing and guiding your child through each page. To a child love is spelled T-I-M-E. Relationship is everything. Enjoy your kids.

**Look for opportunities to practice and reinforce the ideals presented on these pages.**
Perfect practice makes perfect. You cannot just preach to your children and expect them to live godly lives. The best example for your child is your example. As you go through your routines of each day, look for opportunities for you and your child to put into practice the principles and truths read about in the *Treasure of Trust*. Remember, it is not just about you, it is about them.

# THE TREASURE OF TRUST

"Yipee, it's Saturday!" Jules jumps out of bed and twirls around with Cuddles in her hands. "I am so excited. Today, I'm going on a treasure hunt with my best friend, Toby, and his little sister, Ruby," Jules says to Cuddles.

Jules' grandfather calls her. She quickly dresses and runs into the kitchen.

Poppy says, "Good morning, Jules. Your breakfast is ready."

Jules inhales deeply. "It smells yummy, Poppy, but I don't have time for breakfast. Toby and Ruby are coming over and we're going to search for hidden treasure."

Smiling, Poppy plops a big scoop of cinnamon oatmeal into Jules' bowl and pours her a big glass of apple juice. "I think you have time. You need lots of energy to find hidden treasure," he tells her.

Jules giggles and sits down at the table. She rubs her tummy and says with a grin, "I guess I am a little hungry."

"Good girl, you eat breakfast and I'll pack lunches for you and your friends," says Poppy.

11

Knock...knock...knock, Jules runs to the door and flings it open. Toby, Jules' best friend, and his little sister, Ruby, rush in.

In a loud and impatient voice, Toby says, "Come on, Jules, we need to go now!"

Jules puts her hands on her hips and replies, "Toby Brown, why are you always in such a hurry? I had to eat breakfast so I would have energy. We have plenty of time."

13

Toby, Jules, and Ruby gather their backpacks loaded with supplies and goodies for their adventure.

"Bye-bye!" they shout as they skip out the door.

Standing at the screen door, Poppy says, "Be safe and take care of each other."

The children, running down the sidewalk, glance back at the house and say, "We will, we will!"

"This is going to be great!" says Toby.

"Yeah" Ruby replies. "I wonder what kind of treasure we'll find today?"

"I don't know, but I can't wait to find out." Jules answers.

"Hey, there's the woods!" Toby shouts as he takes off running. Ruby and Jules speed up to stay close behind him.

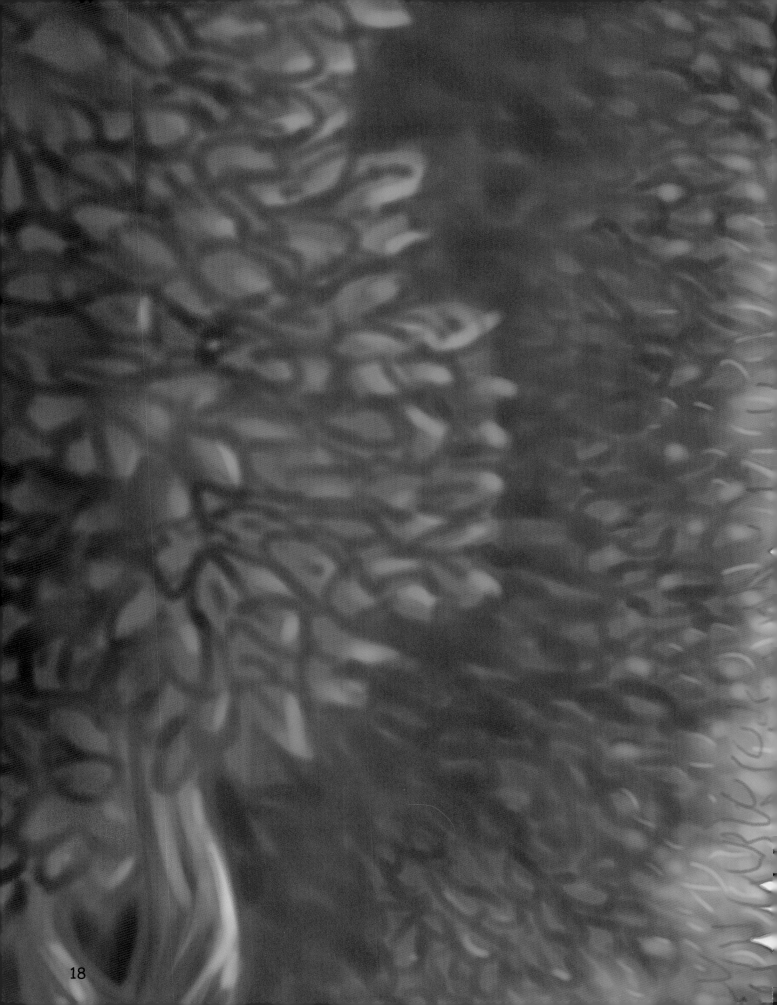

Without warning, Toby suddenly comes to a complete stop. Jules runs **SMACK** into Toby and Ruby runs **SMACK** into Jules. The three stand frozen as they look at a very narrow path that leads into the dark woods.

Ruby, swallowing hard, says, "Maybe we should find another place to look for treasure. Or, maybe we should find a wider path."

Toby, in his bravest voice, replies, "No, sis, this is where the treasure is and this is the only path that leads to it."

Toby, now the self-appointed leader of the exposition, steps onto the path first.  Jules takes Ruby's hand and they follow closely behind.

The sunlight peeks through the trees and lights the pathway and the children relax.

"This isn't so scary after all!" They sing as they dance their way along the path.  "This is a perfect day for a treasure hunt."

Suddenly, Toby stops again. The path ahead splits in two. One path leads to the left, the other leads right. Which way should they go? Then, in the distance, something from the path on the right catches Jules' attention. A beautifully colored rainbow streams from the sky and seems to land in the middle of the trees.

Jules points to the rainbow. "Let's go this way!" she exclaims.

"Yea," agrees Ruby. "I bet there's treasure under those colors. But look how far up the hill it is. Do you think we can make it?"

"Sure, we can make it," says Toby.  He looks at his little sister and realizes that she is already starting to get tired.  "Climb on my back and I'll carry you up the hill," he offers.  Always happy about a horsy back ride from her big brother, Ruby climbs on Toby's back.

Seeing that Toby has a full load, Jules grabs his backpack and carries it for him.  Toby smiles at her and nods appreciatively.

Together, the three of them begin the climb up the hill to the rainbow's end.

After much climbing, the trio finally reaches their goal and find themselves under the rays of the rainbow. Toby and Jules begin to dance and sing, "Rainbow, rainbow, a promise from above. Rainbow, rainbow, a sign of unending love." They become dizzy from dancing round and round, and fall to the ground with a big **THUMP**! They just lay there for a minute as the colors of the rainbow illuminate their faces.

Just then, Ruby squeals in delight! "Come quickly, come quickly!" she calls.

Toby and Jules jump to their feet and run to Ruby. They can't believe their eyes. Right in front of them is a huge treasure chest full of sparkling, colored jewels.

"We're rich!" shouts Toby, jumping up in the air and clicking his heels.

"I'm not so sure," Jules replies. "These gems are different; I've never seen anything like them before." She lifts one out of the chest and shows it to her friends. "They all have writing on them. Look, this one has the word TRUST written on it."

Ruby picks out another jewel and shows Toby. "Look at this one! What does it say, brother?"

"This one says pur...purp...PURPOSE!" he exclaims proudly after sounding out such a long word.

Jules asks, "What should we do now?"

Just then, Ruby's tummy growls very loudly. Toby laughs and answers, "Well, Ruby's tummy says we should eat lunch!"

Giggling, Jules opens her backpack and takes out the lunches and the picnic blanket Poppy packed. She is hungry, too, and glad to see that Poppy packed a lot of food. She takes out four peanut butter and jelly sandwiches, seven chocolate chip cookies, a bag of carrot and celery sticks, and eight apple juice boxes. The three children agree that Poppy packed a picnic feast.

As they begin to eat, something flies over their heads with a SWOOSH and lands with a THUMP near the picnic blanket. Another SWOOSH and THUMP leaves a stone just inches from Ruby.

Toby jumps to his feet, bravely stepping in front of the girls, and shouts in his toughest voice, "Who's there?"

A boy pushes through the bushes and apologetically answers, "I'm so sorry, I didn't know anyone else was here. Is everyone okay? My name is Nathan, I live on the other side of the woods."

Toby stands up very tall and says, "My name is Toby, this is my best friend, Jules, and this is my little sister, Ruby. And yes, we're all okay."

Nathan smiles and says, "Hi." Just then his tummy growls much more loudly than Ruby's had growled earlier and everyone laughs. Jules invites him to join them for lunch. "We have more than enough," she says.

Nathan sits next to Jules, picks up a carrot and says, "I see you've found the hidden treasure of My Kingdom Pals."  He starts to speak again when Ruby interrupts.

"The Kingdom Pals?  What is a Kingdom Pal?" she asks.

Toby, feeling very much the big brother, scolds her.  "Ruby, you know you aren't suppose to interrupt when some is talking."

Ruby apologizes and asks for Nathan's forgiveness.  He smiles at her and says, "The Kingdom Pals are special friends of God.  He uses them to teach us truths about His holy kingdom."  Nathan reaches in the treasure chest and pulls out a jewel with the word HUMILITY written on it.  He puts it in Ruby's hand and whispers in her ear.  "It takes a big person to be humble and ask for forgiveness," he says.

Jules looks at Nathan and asks, "Why do these jewels have words written on them?  And, now that we've found them, are we going to be rich?"

Nathan laughs and replies, "These jewels are very special and are worth more than diamonds and sapphires.  They are **treasure truth** jewels.  God placed them here so we can all learn the truths about His kingdom.  They all have special words on them.  These words remind us that with God's help, ordinary kids like you and me, can do extraordinary things.

Ruby looks confused and asks Toby, "What does extraordinary mean?"

Toby smiles.  "It means super-dooper.  You know, like, things kids think are too big or too tough to do on our own."

"Oh", squeals Ruby.  "Now I get it!"

Nathan continues, "Today, I was practicing the treasure truth of trust, just like my Kingdom Pal, David, did thousands of years ago. Actually, that's why I'm dressed like this and that's why I was slinging stones with this slingshot. Boy, I sure am glad I didn't hurt anyone while you were eating lunch. Hey, let me show you my Kingdom Pal, David. I put him in the treasure chest this morning while I was practicing the slingshot."

Nathan digs down into the treasure chest and pulls out a stuffed toy. He holds it up and says, "Ah-ha, I found him. This is my Kingdom Pal, David."

38

David begins to move and talk.  Turning to Nathan, he says, "Hi, buddy.
Who are your friends?"

Ruby squeals with delight and claps her hands.  Nathan introduces David to each of his
new friends.  David says to them, "It's nice to meet you.  I'm Nathan's Kingdom Pal, but
I want to be your pal, too.  We can have a great time getting to know each other.  Would
you like to know how I discovered my treasure truth jewel, trust?"

"Yes, yes, yes!" the children say in unison.

Then David says, "Okay, but I'm going to need your help.  I need you to use your
imagination so that I can take you to where I received my first treasure jewel.  Every
body ready?  Let's go!"

Suddenly Jules, Ruby, Toby, Nathan and David are plucked out of the woods and into a pasture full of sheep.

"This is unbelievable!" Toby says. "Where are we?"

"This is where I watch over my father's sheep," David explains. "Follow me," he calls, as he motions with his hand.

David asks the children, "Do you ever have problems that seem bigger than you can handle? I always did, it just seemed like it was one thing after another. It was during one of those times when I discovered the treasure truth jewel, Trust."

Ruby looks at her brother and, before she can ask, Toby explains. "To trust is to depend on, or believe in, or know something for sure." Ruby smiles and nods her head. David goes on with his story.

My job as a shepherd wasn't easy.  It was hard to sit in the hot sun all day and watch the sheep.  Sometimes it got really boring.  But, my father depended on me and I knew that even when it seemed that my job wasn't very important, it really was.  Sometimes, my job could be very exciting and a little scary.  You see, sometimes sheep wander away from the flock and, as a shepherd, I had to leave the flock just to find that one sheep. I never knew what kind of trouble that one sheep might be in.   Just like one time when..."

At that very moment, Ruby screams, "WOLF, WOLF, WOLF!"

In one swift movement, David turns, puts a stone in his slingshot, and hurls the stone toward the wolf, which runs away in fear. "That's just what I was telling you. Things like that happened all the time. It took a lot of practice to learn how to hit a moving target using a slingshot. At first, I would miss, or drop the rock or the slingshot. I was afraid that the wolf, or the lion, or the bear would come after me, too. But, I prayed to God and asked Him to help me. With each prayer, I was surer that He would help me and I got better and better at using the slingshot. I began to realize that God could be counted on for every problem in my life, not just with protecting the sheep.

44

He placed special words in my heart that really helped me....**When I listen and obey, I can always trust God to do exactly what He says He will do.** My treasure truth jewel, trust, helps to remind me to trust in God. He helps me do things I can't do on my own and protects me from danger. Trusting in Him also gives me courage and helps me to be brave even when I am afraid. And, praying to God is the key to learning to trust in Him. Since I spent a lot of time out in this pasture alone, I prayed a lot. Sometimes I wrote songs to praise Him. Would you like to hear one?"

"Oh, yes!" the children answer.

David begins to sing.

"Even when I am afraid,
I keep on trusting you.
I praise your promises!
I trust you and am not afraid.
No one can harm me."

"As my trust in God grew stronger, He gave me more important things to do for Him," David explains. My older brothers were in the army and one day my father sent me to visit them and take them some good food. When I arrived at their camp, all of the soldiers, including my brothers, were afraid and upset. You see, there was an enemy soldier, a Philistine, who was a giant. When I say giant, I don't mean that he was just kind of tall. I mean he was a GIANT and stood almost TEN feet tall!"

"Wow, what did you do? Did you run away?" asked the children.

"No, I didn't run, although all the other soldiers did. This giant, whose name was Goliath, made me mad. He was loud and smelly and mean, but worse than that, he was making fun of my God!"

"I just couldn't stand it anymore.  I prayed and decided to trust God and I told King Saul that I would fight Goliath myself.  I remembered all the times God gave me victories over the lion, the wolf, and the bear.  I trusted that God would give me a victory over Goliath, as well.  I walked out to meet Goliath on the battlefield, with no armor except for my slingshot.

When Goliath saw me, I must have looked like an ant to him.  He started laughing and he called me a little boy.  He told me he would squish me like a bug!  I just kept praying for God's help and I ran toward Goliath with my loaded slingshot.  I swung my slingshot as hard as I could.  The stone hit Goliath and he fell to the ground with a loud CRASH!

Then the soldiers and I all celebrated and praised God for the victory!

Lifting her arms in the air, Ruby shouted, "Ya-hoo! That was great!"

Smiling, Nathan lifts David off his lap. In a flash they are back in the rainbow clearing with the treasure chest. As he puts David back into the chest, Nathan says, "When you trust God, He'll give you victories, too."

"How do you know that?" Toby asks Nathan.

Patting Toby on the shoulder, Nathan answers, "I have trusted God for myself. I know what He can do. I've never had to fight lions or bears, but other problems can be just as scary."

"Tell us about it; tell us about how God helped you!" cry Jules and Ruby.

"I'd be glad to," replies Nathan.

"At my school, most of the kids look pretty much like me," Nathan begins.

"You mean they all have red hair?" asks Ruby as Toby and Jules giggle.

"No, I mean that most everyone has my ethnic background, you know, skin color.  Anyway, there is a girl who came to my school this year from a far away country.   She can't speak English very well and she looks very different from the rest of us.  Even the clothes she wears are really different from ours.  Her name is Tawmeem.  A lot of the kids talk about her and make fun of her.  They start rumors about her and her family that aren't true.  She just always looks so sad."

"She fell and broke her leg a few weeks ago and my teacher asked me if I could help her carry her books while she was in her cast.  I said yes and it turns out that Tawmeem is a very nice person.  So, I asked her to sit at my table at lunch.  Well, all of my friends got mad at me for that and they moved to another table.  They would all sit and point and laugh at us while we ate.  I tried to ignore them but it was pretty hard.  I wanted to be with my friends, but I liked Tawmeem and she had become my friend, too."

"The school bully really gave me a hard time. He pushed me with his shoulder when he passed me in the hall and called me some bad names.

He said some very bad things to Tawmeem, and when I told him to knock it off, he tried to get me to fight him.

I went home on Friday, not knowing what to do, and I prayed as hard as I have ever prayed. This bully is a lot bigger than I am and I knew that he could really hurt me if he wanted to. I was afraid to go back to school on Monday."

"I would play sick and stay home if that happened to me," says Jules. Toby and Ruby nod in agreement.

"Believe me, I wanted to," replies Nathan. "But I felt God was telling me that everything would be okay. So, off to school I went."

"When I got to school on Monday morning, I noticed a group of kids gathered in the hall. They were laughing and making fun of someone. I was afraid that it was Tawmeem, so I wiggled inside the group. To my surprise, it was the school bully. He had a bicycle wreck over the weekend and had knocked out four of his front teeth. He also cut his head and had to have stitches and the doctor had to shave part of his hair in order to sew him up. He did look funny! And when he yelled at the kids to leave him alone, he sounded funny, too!

"Thop it, thop it.  Thop making fun of me!"  he said with a terrible lisp.

"I started to laugh, too, until I felt God tugging on my heart.  I walked over to the bully and told him that it was okay.  I said that his hair would grow back, and that his teeth could be fixed.  That day, at lunch, he asked if he could sit with Tawmeem and me.  The three of us are now great friends and he doesn't bully anymore because he now knows how it hurts to be teased.  God helped me, and God taught him a good life lesson, as well.

"That's amazing how that worked out," says Toby.

"God is amazing," answers Nathan as Jules and Ruby reflect on the story they've just heard.

"Do you have any other Kingdom Pals who can tell us stories?" asks Ruby.

Nathan digs in the treasure chest and pulls out the other Kingdom Pals along with the treasure truth jewels he discovered with them.

> Moses, Leadership
> Esther, Purpose
> Joseph, Forgiveness
> Daniel, Prayer
> Mary, Faith
> Matthew, Loyalty

And, of course!
> Jesus, Love

Toby, again being the grown-up big brother, says to Ruby. "Ruby, I would love to stay and hear about all of these, too, but we better be getting home. It's getting late."

"Can we meet him here another day?" Ruby asks Toby.

"Sure you can!" says Nathan. "I can't wait till I see you guys again!"

"Thank you," they reply. The new friends hug good-bye.

As Nathan hugs Jules, he whispers in her ear, "I put something special in your backpack for you."

LEADERSHIP    PURPOSE    FORGIVENESS

PRAYER    FAITH    LOYALTY    LOVE    55

Jules runs in the house, slamming the front screen door and calling out. "Poppy, Poppy, I'm home!"

Poppy answers, "Did you find your treasure?  Are we now rich?" he winks at Jules.

"Well, yes and no.  We found treasure all right, but it was Kingdom Pals treasure."

"Who are the Kingdom Pals, Jules?"  Poppy asks.

Jules climbs in Poppy's lap, snuggles in his arms and tells him all about her day.

"The Kingdom Pals are very special toys.  They are not like any other toy I have ever seen before. They are soft, lovable and very, very cute. There's David, Jesus, Moses, Mary, Joseph and more  They have a very special job to do.  They help ordinary kids like me and my friends live extraordinary lives by teaching us about God's word."

Poppy taps a worn burgundy book on the table next to his chair. "Dumplin," he calls Jules, "those Kingdom Pals are the same people I read about in this Bible everyday.  The Kingdom Pals can teach you a lot about God through their stories."

"Really?" says Jules, happily.

That night, as she gets ready for bed, Jules smiles and remembers her day.  She reaches in her backpack and pulls out a treasure truth jewel she had wrapped carefully in a napkin.  On the back of the jewel, she reads this message:

A Jewel for Your Journey

Lord, help me to trust in you
when problems come my way;
I know I'll have the victory,
when I trust you and obey!"

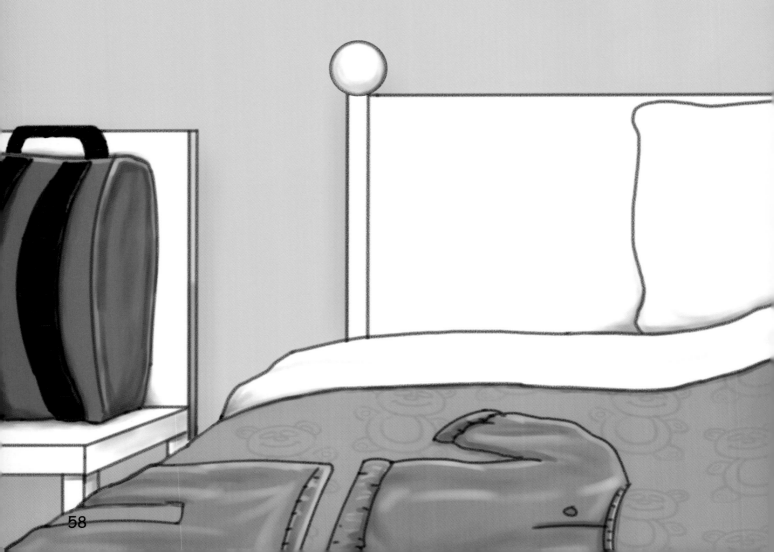

Just then, Jules remembers that Nathan told her he put a special surprise in her backpack. She reaches in it again and feels something soft and fury. When she pulls it out, she squeals with delight! It is Nathan's Kingdom Pal, David. Along with it is a note that reads, "Whenever you are afraid, trust in God."

Jules smiles and places David on her bed next to Cuddles. She says, "Cuddles, meet my Kingdom Pal, David."

# Just For Parents, Teachers and Caregivers

**And all thy children [shall be] taught of the LORD;
and great [shall be] the peace of thy children.  Isa. 54:13**

Imagine that you allow your child, for the first time, to go with a group of his friends for an afternoon trip downtown.  Along the way, your child is distracted and strays from his group.  Somewhat alarmed, he starts walking, but in the opposite direction than his group.  After a couple of turns, he realizes he is in a place he has never been.  He starts to walk a little faster now.  It is getting cold and the sky is growing darker.  It starts to rain.  Your child continues to walk alone down the unfamiliar street.

At home, you are a little concerned since this is his first trip downtown without you.  However, you take comfort in the fact that you packed all he could possibly need in his backpack before he left home.  As time passes, you begin to doubt yourself and take a mental inventory of his supplies.

Your child now finds himself at a dead end street.  He stops.  He's cold, hungry and frightened.  The narrow alley is growing dark as the sun begins to set.  He removes the backpack he is carrying and remembers he argued about taking it with him.  Now he is glad he listened to you.  He reaches in the backpack, and finds a small flashlight.  With the light illuminating the darkness, he reaches into the backpack again.  This time he pulls out a thick sweater and an umbrella.  He puts his hand in the backpack a third time, hoping that he would find something to eat and he pulls out a sandwich and bottle of water.  He smiles as he sits it down next to him.  He reaches in one more time and smiles again as he pulls out the cell phone he hoped you included.  As he dials your number, he says a quiet prayer of thanks.  "Thank you Lord, for my parents that gave me everything I need to survive in this strange place".

It is now dark and you are truly worried.  The phone rings and you pick up immediately, answering as calmly as you can.  On the other end is the voice of your child, calm, cool and collected.

"Can you come and pick me up?  I got a little lost and I'm at a place I've never been before.  And, thanks for making me bring this backpack.  It's amazing that you packed everything I needed".

You smile to yourself and say a quiet prayer.  "Thank you, Lord, for supplying me with everything I needed and directing me to put it in his backpack."

Our children go into the world and face the variety of challenges life presents.  Every moment of every waking hour, they are faced with choices.  Therefore, we must pack their "spiritual backpacks" with everything they may possibly need.  What we instill in them is what will determine if they are adequately equipped to handle those challenges to their best advantage and to the glory of God.

It is the light of God's word that you implant in your child's heart that will help him find his way in a dark and troubled world.  It is a personal relationship with God, through his son, Jesus, that will bring him comfort and warmth when the storms of life rage.  It is the word of God that will satisfy his hunger and cause him to never thirst.  It is the confidence that he can enter into the throne room of the Most High through prayer and ask for grace in his time of need that will bring him home safe.  It is the spiritual legacy you pass on to your child that will become his greatest asset.

It is the purpose of this book, and My Kingdom Pals™ ministry resources, to equip you with the tools you need to help you put the word of God in the hands and hearts of your children.  So, when the battles of life rage, they are prepared to correctly respond to every challenge.

## Ministry Moments

Each page of this book is loaded with opportunities to add needed supplies to your child's spiritual backpack. You can use "The Hidden Treasures of My Kingdom Pals Series" as a daily or weekly family time devotional, during story time, or when you tuck your little one into bed.

The following pages reveal the hidden treasures of "The Treasure of Trust". They present opportunities and ideas that go beyond the words of the text to minister to the heart of your child. These pages also offer ideas on how to practice these truths in your everyday walk. We often talk and lecture our children about right and wrong, but many of us have found this to be ineffective. The Bible has the answer to this problem. It says, in Proverbs 22:6, "Train up a child in the way he should go and when he is old, he will not depart from it."

Webster's defines training as "**to prepare for a challenge, to direct the growth of an individual, to form by instruction, discipline, or drill. It is to make one fit and qualified. Prepared (as by exercise) for a test of skill.**" How do we train up our children? We prepare them for the challenges of life, we direct their growth, and we form them by instruction, discipline and drills. We do what we can to make them qualified for the Kingdom of God. We pray and prepare them for the greatest test of all...the test of life.

We must also practice the truths of God's word and His statutes until they are perfected in ourselves and our children. Don't be alarmed by the word "perfected". In the New Testament, "perfect" is often translated from a Greek word which means, "to make one what he ought to be". And, our job is to equip our children with what they need so they can become all God has destined them to be.

As you go through "The Treasure of Trust", first, read the page then ask your child what they see on the page. As they point out different thoughts and illustrations, relate them to truths from God's word. We provide many ministry opportunities for you. If your child has questions, we suggest that you look in the Bible as you answer. This trains your child to do the same when he faces issues he can't readily discern. Also, if your child doesn't participate with his individual ideas at first, understand that this is normal and don't push too hard. You lead the discussion; you point out the different illustrations and introduce new ideas. Your child will catch on quickly and will participate with you before you know it. If you have My Kingdom Pal™, David, use him to narrate the story. Let him interact with your child as he leads them to the hidden treasures of My Kingdom Pals. Allow him to take your child back in time when he was a keeper of his father's sheep. When story time is over, hand David to your child and watch your child continue to develop an even deeper relationship with the things of God while interacting and playing with David. Be sure to review the Bible verse on the bottom of David. Remind your child that David was afraid many times and that learning to trust God helped his fear and will help his, too.

The remainder of this section is a "Parent's Eye View of the Treasure of Trust". In it you will find illustrative references to guide you through the accompanying Ministry Moments. We have also included scriptural references to support the ministry moments as well as training exercises to help reinforce them. To make it easier for you, these have been done in 2 to 4 page groupings. Enjoy the process of discovery with your child. Remember, to a child love is spelled T-I-M-E.

### Page Group 8-11

### Illustrative Reference
- The whale poster (pg. 8)
- The birds singing in the tree, the butterflies, the flowers, the tree (pg. 9)
- The bowl of oatmeal and the bags of lunch that Poppy is packing (pg. 10)

## Ministry Moment
- God created all things on the earth.
- You are a special gift from God
- The importance of taking care of your body because the Holy Spirit lives in it.

## Scripture References
- Gen. 1:1:  In the beginning God created the heaven and the earth.
- Psalms 127:3:  Lo, children [are] an heritage of the LORD: [and] the fruit of the womb [is his] reward.
- 1Chr. 3:16:  Know ye not that ye are the temple of God, and [that] the Spirit of God dwelleth in you?

## Training Exercise
The next time you are out walking with your child, point to a tree and ask, "Who made that?"  Point to a bird and ask, "Who made that?"  Point to yourself and ask, "Who made me?" Point to your child and ask, "Who made you?"  Tell him that God made him special and there is no body else in the whole world like him.

At snack time, ask your child to pick a healthy snack.  If he can't choose one on his own, help him make a good choice.  Ask, "Why is it important to eat healthy snacks?"  This same exercise can be used while bathing, dressing, going to school, taking medicine, or anytime taking good care of the body is appropriate.

Of course, the answer is God for the first training exercise.  For the second exercise, the answer is "because our body is the temple of God, we must take extra special care of it".  When a correct answer is given, celebrate! Give him a high five, jump up, and get excited! If he doesn't get it right the first time, gently inform him of the right answer and play the training game over again until he understands. Don't condemn, don't tear down, and don't criticize.  Encourage, edify and uplift.

Page Group 12-15

## Illustrative Reference
- Toby (pg. 13)
- Everyone  Welcome Sign (pg. 14)
- The garden (pg. 14)
- The bag of seeds (pg. 14)
- Toby holding Ruby's hand (pg. 14)

## Ministry Moment
- Patience is something that must be practiced.
- Love your neighbor as yourself.
- Everyone is welcome in heaven.
- You reap what you sew.

## Scripture References
- 1Sam 12:16:  Now therefore stand and see this great thing, which the LORD will do before your eyes
- Hebrews 6:12:  We do not want you to become lazy, but to imitate those who through faith and patience inherit what has been promised.
- Mark 12:31:  And the second [is] like, [namely] this, Thou shalt love thy neighbour as thyself. There is none other commandment greater than these.
- John 3:16:  For God so loved the world, that he gave his only begotten Son, that whosoever believeth in him should not perish, but have everlasting life.
- 1 John 4:11: Beloved, if God so loved us, we ought also to love one another.
- Gal 6:7:  Be not deceived; God is not mocked: for whatsoever a man soweth, that shall he also reap.

## Training Exercise
The next time your child demands your presence and the situation is not urgent, encourage him to "Practice Patience" and tell him "those who are willing to wait well are usually the ones who get what has been promised to them".

Have special set apart days called "Acts of Kindness Day".  Encourage your children to look for opportunities to be kind, to show mercy and generosity, and to offer hospitality.  Do this often and reward them for their efforts.

Top off your "Acts of Kindness Day" with a trip to the library or ice cream shop, maybe even a movie or some other special family outing or activity. If you have more than one child, encourage a contest. Imagine your kids competing over who will be the most kind, generous and merciful! This would definitely be a win…win…win situation. Remember, don't condemn, don't tear down, and don't criticize. Encourage, edify and uplift. Make these training days fun for your entire household.

## Page Group 16-19

### Illustrative Reference
- The children running. (pgs. 16-17)
- Ruby. (pg. 19)

### Ministry Moment
- Follow after the things of God
- Dealing with and overcoming fear

### Scriptural Reference
- 1 Timothy 6:11-12: But thou, O man of God, flee these things; and follow after righteousness, godliness, faith, love, patience, meekness.
- 1Ti 6:12 Fight the good fight of faith, lay hold on eternal life, whereunto thou art also called, and hast professed a good profession before many witnesses.
- Hebrews 12:1: Wherefore seeing we also are compassed about with so great a cloud of witnesses, let us lay aside every weight, and the sin which doth so easily beset [us], and let us run with patience the race that is set before us,
- 1 John 4:18: There is no fear in love; but perfect love casteth out fear: because fear hath torment. He that feareth is not made perfect in love.
- 1 John 4:4: Ye are of God, little children, and have overcome them: because greater is he that is in you, than he that is in the world.
- 2 Timothy 1:1: For God hath not given us the spirit of fear; but of power, and of love, and of a sound mind.

### Training Exercise
Create opportunities for him to make good choices. When he makes a good choice, celebrate it. When he doesn't, gently inform him of the correct way.

Talk about things that may be scary to your children and tell them how God has protected others and how he will protect them too. Tell them about an actual time in your life when God protected you. If a fearful situation occurs, use it for a moment of ministry. Stop and pray with them. Guide them on how to trust God and look to God in all situations. Every moment is vital in training our children so never waste any opportunity. Remember, don't condemn, don't tear down, and don't criticize. Encourage, uplift and edify.

## Page Group 20-23

### Illustrative Reference
- The path and the beauty of the day. (pg. 20-21)
- The easy path, the not so easy path, and the hills and obstacles of the not so easy path. (pg. 23-24)

### Ministry Moment
- God will lead, protect and sustain you.
- God's way may not always be the easiest way, but it is always the best way.

### Scriptural Reference
- Psalms 23:2: He maketh me to lie down in green pastures: he leadeth me beside the still waters
- 1 Peter 5:7: Casting all your care upon him; for he careth for you.
- Exodus. 14:14: The LORD shall fight for you, and ye shall hold your peace

### Training Exercise
Take your child on a walk or simply out in the yard. Have him listen to the beautiful sounds of God's creation and the beautiful colors He placed in nature.

Talk to your child about the importance of doing things God's way. Give them examples of how God's way is sometimes the harder way, i.e. telling the truth even when it means he might be punished for doing something wrong. Explain how God's way is the lasting, eternal way and the only path to follow.

## Page Group 24-27

### Illustrative Reference
- Toby carries Ruby while Jules carries Toby's backpack. (pg. 25)
- Treasure chest and the rainbow. (pgs 26-27)

### Ministry Moment
- Ask, "What does it mean to love your neighbor as yourself"? "Who is your neighbor"? "What are some ways to show this kind of love"?
- God's Promises
- Accomplishing Goals (Diligence rewarded)

### Scriptural References
- John 13:35: By this shall all [men] know that ye are my disciples, if ye have love one to another
- Prov. 13:4: The soul of the sluggard desireth, and [hath] nothing: but the soul of the diligent shall be made fat.

### Training Exercise
This is another opportunity to have a "Special Acts of Kindness Day". See Ministry Moments for pages 12-15.

## Page Group 28-31

### Illustrative Reference
- Treasure chest and jewels. (pgs. 28-29)
- Toby and Nathan. (pgs. 30-31)

### Ministry Moment
- True treasure
- Being brave

### Scriptural References
- Exodus. 19:5: Now therefore, if ye will obey my voice indeed, and keep my covenant, then ye shall be a peculiar treasure unto me above all people: for all the earth [is] mine:
- Is. 33:6: And wisdom and knowledge shall be the stability of thy times, [and] strength of salvation: the fear of the LORD [is] his treasure.
- Mt. 12: 35: A good man out of the good treasure of the heart bringeth forth good things: and an evil man out of the evil treasure bringeth forth evil things.
- Jos 1:9: Have not I commanded thee? Be strong and of a good courage; be not afraid, neither be thou dismayed: for the LORD thy God [is] with thee whithersoever thou goest.

### Training Exercise
Share with your child the treasures of God's promises. Start teaching at an early age the value of living God's way verses seeking the treasures of this world.

Talk to your child about situations where he might need to be brave even though he is afraid. Stress the importance of trusting in God as David did.

## Page Group 32-35

### Illustrative Reference
- Ruby (pg. 32)
- Nathan (pg. 33)

### Ministry Moment
- The power and importance of humility.
- The power of words.

### Scriptural References
- Prov. 22:4: By humility [and] the fear of the LORD [are] riches, and honour, and life.
- Col. 3:16: Let the word of Christ dwell in you richly in all wisdom; teaching and admonishing one another in psalms and hymns and spiritual songs, singing with grace in your hearts to the Lord.

- Col. 3:17: And whatsoever ye do in word or deed, [do] all in the name of the Lord Jesus, giving thanks to God and the Father by him.
- James 1:22-23: But be ye doers of the word, and not hearers only, deceiving your own selves. For if any be a hearer of the word, and not a doer, he is like unto a man beholding his natural face in a glass.

## Training Exercise

Talk to your child about humility. Ask him to name some situations where he was sorry for something he did. Explain how learning to admit fault and saying "I'm sorry" will help him develop a repentant heart toward God. Stress how quickly and easily God forgives! Remind him that, just as Nathan did, we should be quick to forgive as well.

## Page Group 36-39

### Illustrative Reference
- The picnic lunch. (pgs. 36-37)
- David (pg. 39)

### Ministry Moment
- Hospitality
- David was a real person that lived a long time ago. The Bible tells about his life. What was special about David? David was a man after God's own heart. How? He sought the ways of God. His desire was to be pleasing to the Lord, not to himself and not to man.

### Scriptural Reference
- Rom. 12:13: Distributing to the necessity of saints; given to hospitality.
- 1Peter 4:9: Use hospitality one to another without grudging.
- 1 Sam. 13:14: But now thy kingdom shall not continue: the LORD hath sought him a man after his own heart, and the LORD hath commanded him [to be] captain over his people, because thou hast not kept [that] which the LORD commanded thee.

## Training Exercise

Invite a special guest, grandparent, aunt, uncle, or even other children and teach your child the finer points of being a good host and let him know that this is important to God. Stress to him that serving others is caring for others. Share with him how even God's son, Jesus Christ, served his disciples and others while he was on this earth.

## Page Group 40-43

### Illustrative Reference
- The sheep and David's job as a Shepherd

### Ministry Moment
- We are the sheep and Jesus is our good shepherd

### Scriptural Reference
- John 10:14: I am the good shepherd, and know my [sheep], and am known of mine.

## Training Reference

Make sheep using cotton balls on construction paper and talk about the relationship between a shepherd and his sheep. Explain how just as David's job was taking care of his father's flock and keeping them from harm, so it is with Jesus and his followers. Help him understand that God is always watching over his children.

## Page Group 44-47

### Illustrative References
- The sheep eating grass
- The wolf
- David's countenance
- The Slingshot

### Ministry Moment
- We may not see danger coming, but God is watching over us to protect us.
- Nothing is too difficult for God.
- Don't allow fear to stop you from doing what you know is right.
- God always equips us with what we need for every battle.

### Scriptural Reference
- Luke 1:37:  For with God nothing shall be impossible.
- Psalms 56:3-4:  What time I am afraid, I will trust in thee. In God I will praise his word, in God I have put my trust; I will not fear what flesh can do unto me.

### Training Reference
Take your child into a dark room at night. Reassure him that he can trust you to stay with him.  Then, give him a flashlight and help him turn it on.  Explain that just as you have given him a light with which to see, God gives us the right equipment for our battle.  Also explain that even though your child could not see you in the darkness, he knew you were with him.  Help him understand that even though we cannot see God watching over us, He is always with us and has promised never to leave us alone.

### Page Group 48-51

### Illustrative reference
- Ruby's excitement
- Tawmeen

### Ministry Moment
- The Bible is given to us by God to help us face every issue in life.
- No matter how different we look to each other, we are all the same in God's eyes because He created each of us.

### Scriptural Reference
- Ps.32:8:  I will instruct thee and teach thee in the way which thou shalt go: I will guide thee with mine eye.
- Prov. 4:13:  Take fast hold of instruction; let [her] not go: keep her; for she [is] thy life.
- Gal 3:28:  There is neither Jew nor Greek, there is neither bond nor free, there is neither male nor female: for ye are all one in Christ Jesus.

### Training Exercise
Take your child to a mall, park, etc.  Have him notice how different each person is from another.  Help him to see the beauty in the variety of God's creation.  Now, have him look at different types of flowers.  Have him notice the beauty in the different colors of the flowers.  Then, stress to your child that no person or group of persons is better than another. God made us all beautiful and let your child understand that making fun of someone who looks different from him is to make fun of God's creation.

### Page Group 52-55

### Illustrative Reference
- Nathan (pg. 52)
- The Bully (pg. 52)

### Ministry Moment
- Hearing the voice of God and doing what he says.
- God will fight your battles.
- Pray for people who make fun of you and use you.

### Scriptural Reference
- Deut. 28:1:  And it shall come to pass, if thou shalt hearken diligently unto the voice of the LORD thy God, to observe [and] to do all his commandments which I command thee this day, that the LORD thy God will set thee on high above all nations of the earth:
- Exodus. 14:14:  The LORD shall fight for you, and ye shall hold your peace.
- Mat 5:44:  But I say unto you, Love your enemies, bless them that curse you, do good to them that hate you, and pray for them which despitefully use you, and persecute you.

## Training Exercise

Whether dealing with siblings at home or other children at school, conflicts will arise from time to time. Doing what is right in the sight of God can be quite difficult to discern and carry out even for adults. Take time to sit down with your child and prepare him for these conflicts. Take hypothetical situations and present them to your child. Use the Bible to help present Godly ways to handle these situations. Teach your child routinely the importance of seeking God's will in volatile situations. Teach him how following the crowd can often lead to disaster. Communicate how brave David, Daniel, Esther, Moses, and others in the Bible truly were as they followed God when others did not.

## Page Group 56-59

### Illustrative Reference
- The Bible (pg. 56)
- The Treasure Truth Jewel (pg. 59)

### Ministry Moments
- Bible, the book with all the answers.
- Trusting God

### Scriptural References
- 2 Tim. 3:16: All scripture [is] given by inspiration of God, and [is] profitable for doctrine, for reproof, for correction, for instruction in righteousness.
- Psalms 5:11: But let all those that put their trust in thee rejoice: let them ever shout for joy, because thou defendest them: let them also that love thy name be joyful in thee.

### Training Exercises
Begin teaching Bible verses to your child. Don't try to go for the quantity, but help him understand what the verses mean to his life. Play games like "find the book of Psalms" and let your child become familiar with where the books are located. Pick out a special verse and tell your child how it reminds you of him.

## Page Group 60-61

### Illustrative Reference
- My Kingdom Pal, David (pg. 61)

### Ministry Moment
- Take this opportunity to reinforce that David was a real person in the Bible. Just like your child, he was once little and as he grew up, God used him in amazing ways, as a musician, as a shepherd, as a warrior, as a father and even a king.

### Scriptural references
- David's name is mentioned in the Bible more times than any other person.
- David is first mentioned in the Book of Ruth as the grandson of Obed and Ruth, who were the parents of Jesse, who was David's father. The rest of David's history is found from 1 Samuel 16 to his death and burial in 1 Chronicles 24:16.

### Training Exercise
Read to your child from the Bible about the life of David. Use a children's story time Bible so it will be at the level he can understand and enjoy. Ask your child what characteristics he likes about David. Help him to pray for these same characteristics in himself.

**And thou shalt teach them diligently unto thy children, and shalt talk of them when thou sittest in thine house, and when thou walkest by the way, and when thou liest down, and when thou risest up.**
**Deuteronomy 6:7**

May God Bless you on your journey and grant you many jewels along the way.

# About My Kingdom Pals™

At My Kingdom Pals we have a heart for the Lord and a special love for children.

The bible is very explicit in telling parents the importance
of teaching children to serve the Lord.

My Kingdom Pals products have been developed to provide parents with bible teaching tools. The plush Pals characters not only provide great companions for children, they offer parents a great way to teach. The teaching book series, color/activity book, and music CD complement the plush characters and continue the Kingdom Pals goal of "Putting the Word of God into the Hands and Hearts of Children."

If we want our children to serve the Lord, they should hear about him from us. It is not enough to rely on the church to provide their bible education. As parents, we must reinforce the lessons of the Bible in our homes.

It is extremely important to begin Bible teaching with children early in life, and the My Kingdom Pals ministry is designed to help parents do just that. We believe that a child is never too young to begin hearing about God.

In Mark 9:36 Jesus took a child and had him stand among his disciples. Taking the child in his arms, he said, "Whoever welcomes one of these little children in my name, welcomes me." In this example Jesus illustrated the importance of not only treating children well, but teaching them about Jesus. Children's ministries should be strongly emphasized in our world today, and a primary objective of My Kingdom Pals is to help parents begin sharing the Bible with their children at a very early age.

In Psalms 127:3, the Bible calls children "a heritage from the Lord, a reward to parents." In Matthew 18:5, Jesus said. "Whoever welcomes a little child in my name welcomes me. But if anyone causes one of these little ones to sin, it would be better for him to have a large millstone hung around his neck and to be drowned in the depths of the sea."
As parents and loving adults, God holds us accountable for how we minister to children and how we affect their ability to trust. Jesus further warned that anyone who turns little children away from faith will receive severe punishment.

Welcome to My Kingdom Pals, where we believe in "Putting the Word of God into the Hands and Hearts of Children."

# Final Word

Passing on a solid spiritual heritage to our next generation is our passion and highest calling.  It is our prayer that this book and all the books in <u>The</u> <u>Hidden Treasures of My Kingdom Pals Series</u> will help you to accomplish this vital mission in a way every child will enjoy, understand and remember.

## My Kingdom Pals™ Ministry Resources

David

Joseph

Esther

Jesus

Moses

Mary

Daniel

Matthew

### Bookmark

Joseph

### My Bible Pals Music

### Jewel for the Journey Plaque

### Treasure of Trust Book

### Activity Book

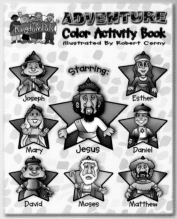

# How to Reach Us

For More Information about My Kingdom Pals™
or to order any of our resources

## Visit us at our Websites

www.mybiblepals.com
www.zoelifepub.com

## Call Us at

My Kingdom Pals™ at (866) 539-7894
ZOE LIFE PUBLISHING at (734) 325-2132

Or

## Write to Us at

My Kingdom Pals™
1006 West Cory Street, Ozark, MO 65721-6403

ZOE LIFE PUBLISHING
P.O. Box 871066, Canton, MI 48187

We would love to hear from you!

Words to Live By